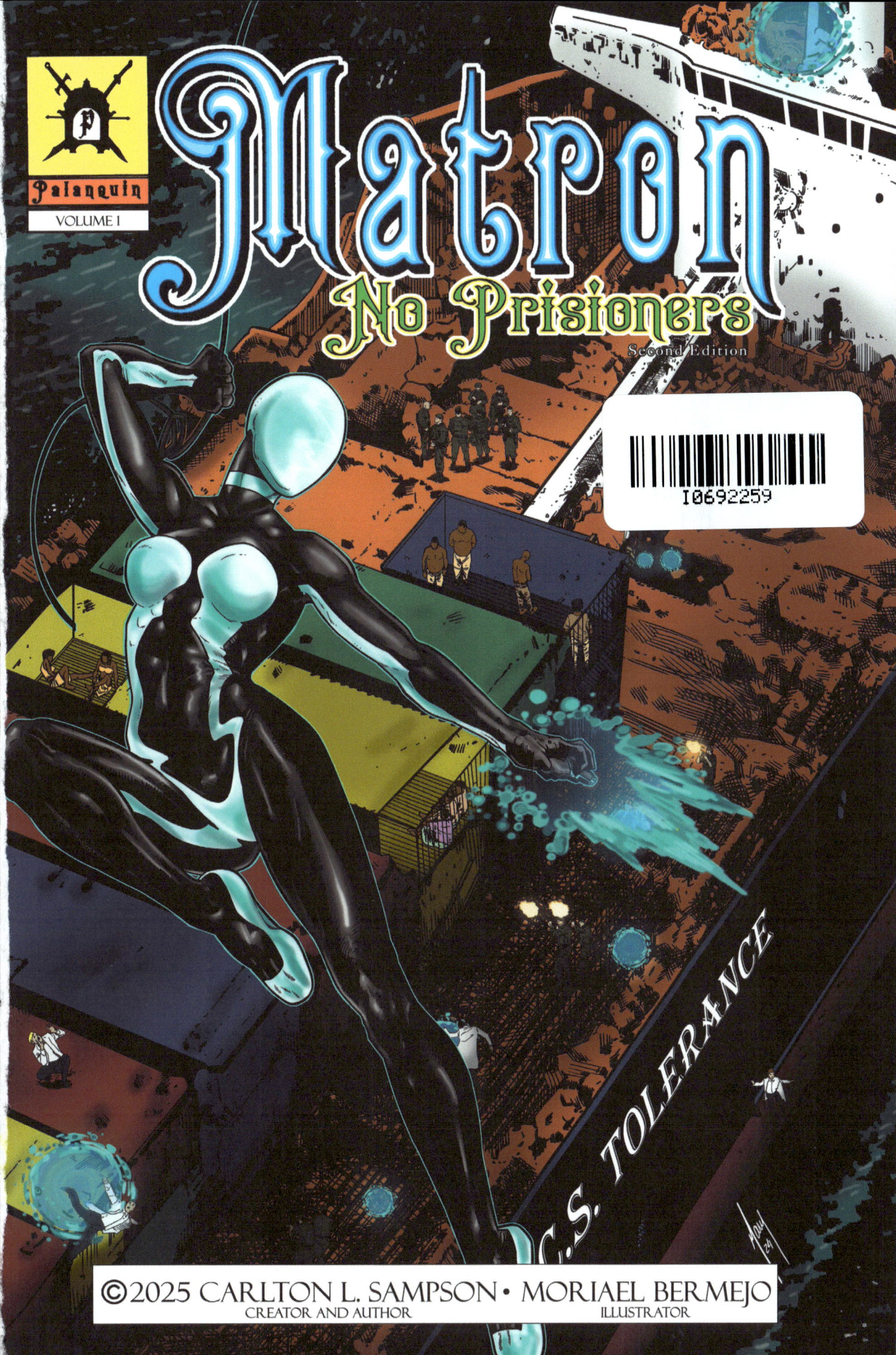

Orney California Wines.

Flavor that transcends, moments that last

For generations the Orney winemakers' family vineyards produced the finest Old World wines. The Orney family's New World vineyards continued the family's tradition of meticulously tended terroirs to produce the finest New World wines.

In 1854 Kristine and Nicolò Orney established their Southern Upper California vineyard. Maintaining the Orney family of winemakers' legacy by meticulously tending terroirs, with traditional techniques to produce some of the finest New World wines.

Orney California Wines.

The wine with the girl on the bottle.

HUMANITY, NO LONGER FEARFUL OF WILD ANIMALS,
THE INNOCENT, OPEN, AND LOVING ARE EASILY MUTUALLY CONTOURED
BY SEXISM, CLASSISM, AND RACISM. ALL JUST VIRTUES OF BELIEF.
EVERYONE LIVES CONSTRAINED, TRAPPED BY SITUATION, AND CONDITIONED
BY ENVIRONMENT AND CULTURAL EXPERIENCE. RACE DOES NOT MATTER.
IT IS ALL ABOUT BREEDING, POSSESSIVENESS, AND IN MATRON'S WORLD,
NATURAL SELECTION, GENERATIONAL WEALTH, AND TIME.
UNLIKE HER PEERS SPENDING THEIR DAYS AND NIGHTS OCCUPYING TIME,
MATRON MINGLES AMONGST THE PEOPLE,
THE MASSES UNDER CORPORATE SERVITUDE AND THE THUMB OF WEALTH.
MATRON'S PASTIME OF CHOICE: DESTROYING MALFEASANT ORGANIZATIONS
BY HUNTING THEIR COLLUDING MALEFACTORS FOR SPORT.
SHE IS MATRON, MATRON ORNEY, OWNER OF ORNEY WINES.
"THE WINE WITH THE GIRL ON THE BOTTLE."

SOCIETIES REQUIRE SUPPORT.
ACTS OF INDIVIDUALS RESOURCING
EFFORTS OF A COMMON GOAL,
MEMBERED GROUPS VALUING A PURPOSE
CHARACTERIZED BY THEIR ACTIONS.

BY DECISION OR CONCESSION GIVEN THE OPPORTUNITY OF CHOICE,

INDIVIDUALS BEAR RESPONSIBILITY FOR THE SUCCESS, FAILURE, OUTCOMES, AND CONSEQUENCES OF THEIR ACTIONS,

WHETHER OR NOT THE CAUSE CONTINUES...

STEVE, EAST WING FRONT CAMERAS 1 AND 2 HAVE DISTORTION ON MY MONITOR.

THAT'S THE ALLEY ENTRANCE. THEY ARE DISTORTED ON MY MONITOR TOO.

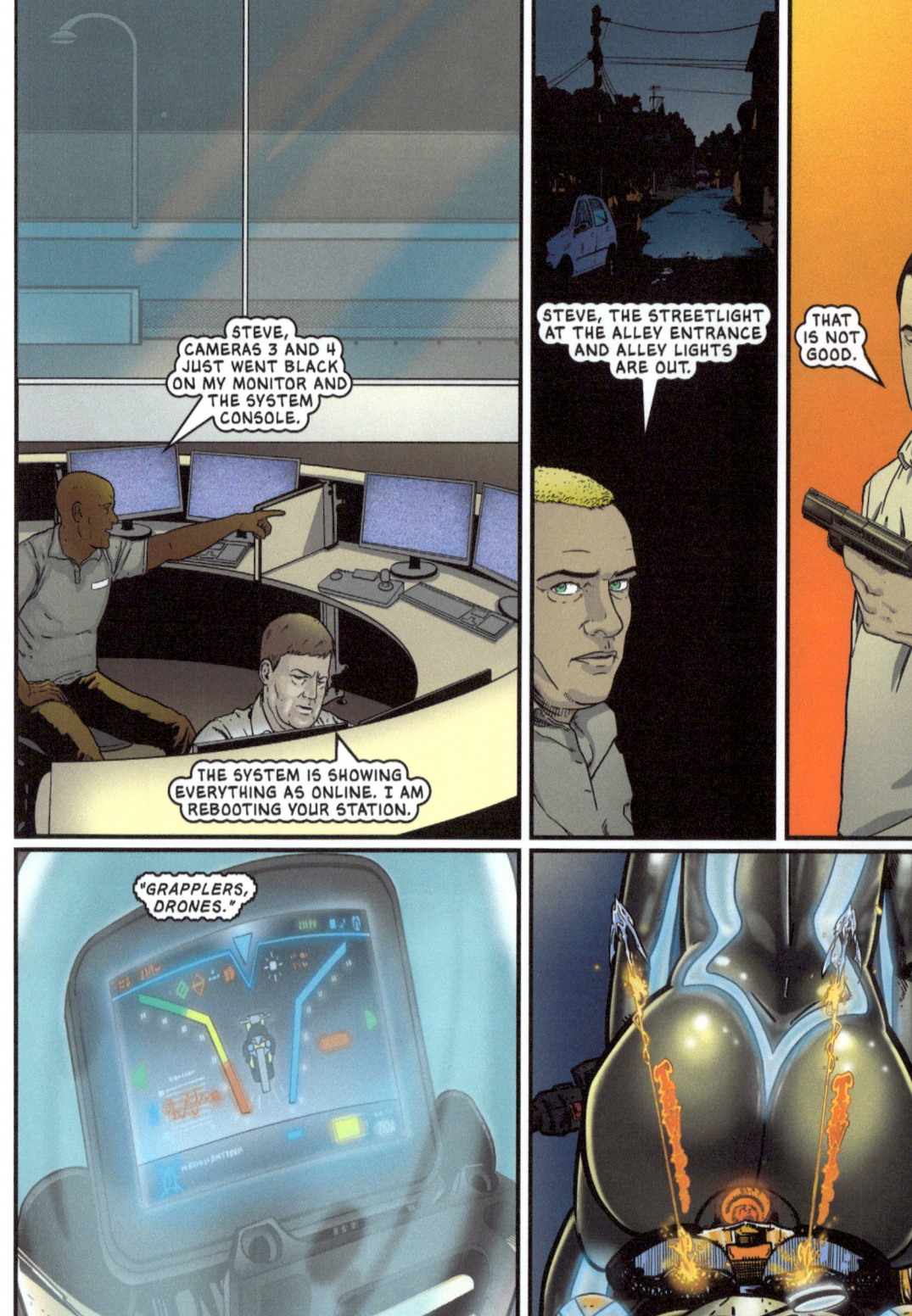

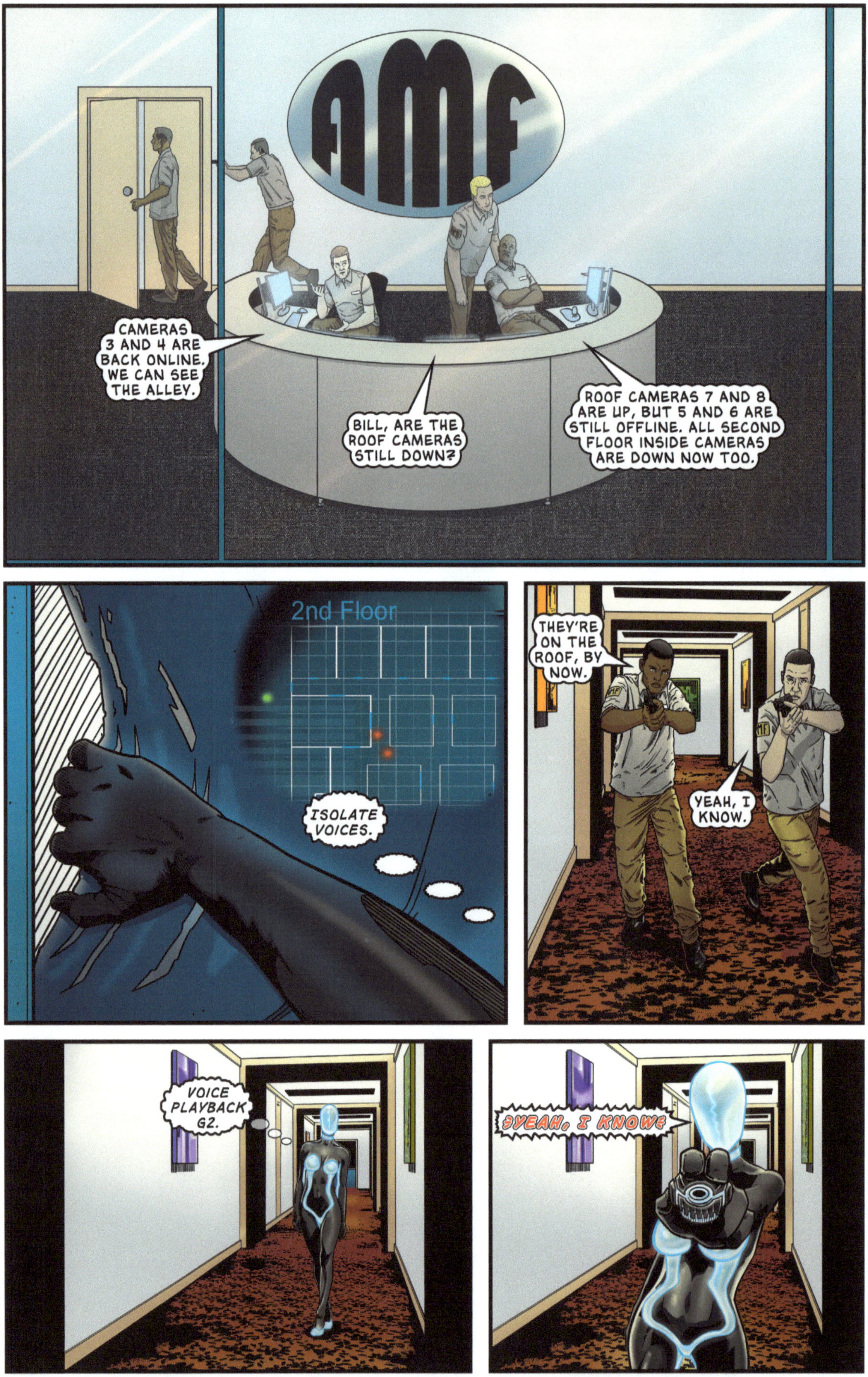

CAMERAS 3 AND 4 ARE BACK ONLINE. WE CAN SEE THE ALLEY.

BILL, ARE THE ROOF CAMERAS STILL DOWN?

ROOF CAMERAS 7 AND 8 ARE UP, BUT 5 AND 6 ARE STILL OFFLINE. ALL SECOND FLOOR INSIDE CAMERAS ARE DOWN NOW TOO.

2nd Floor

ISOLATE VOICES.

THEY'RE ON THE ROOF, BY NOW.

YEAH, I KNOW.

VOICE PLAYBACK G2.

≥YEAH, I KNOW.≥

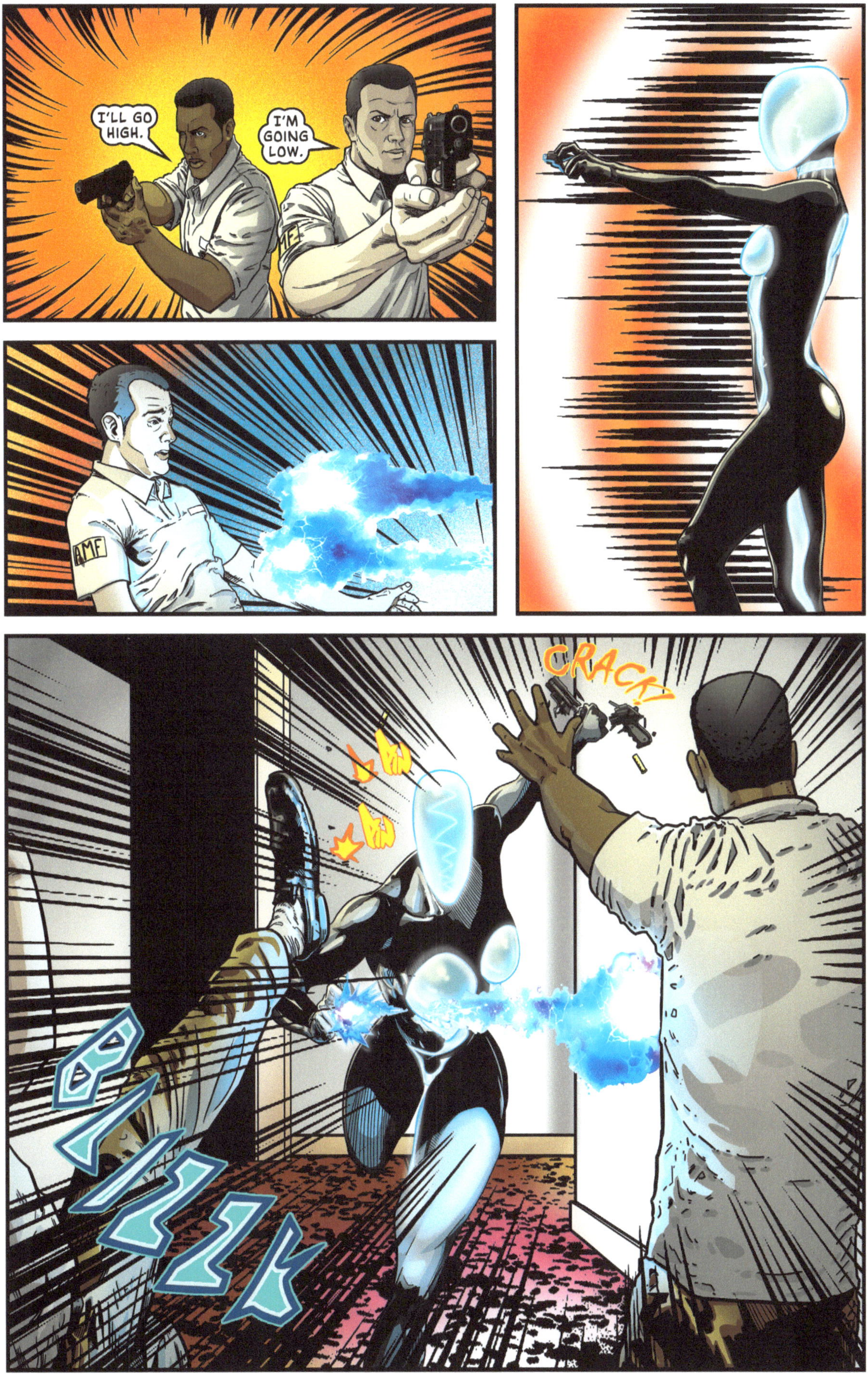

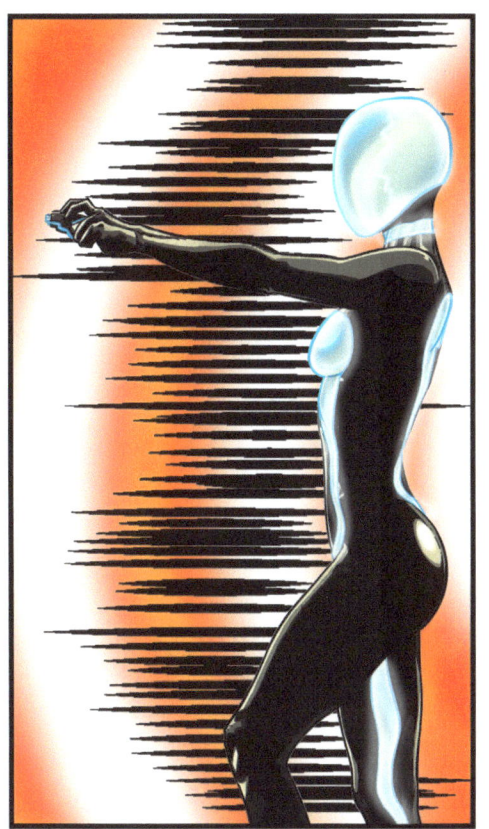

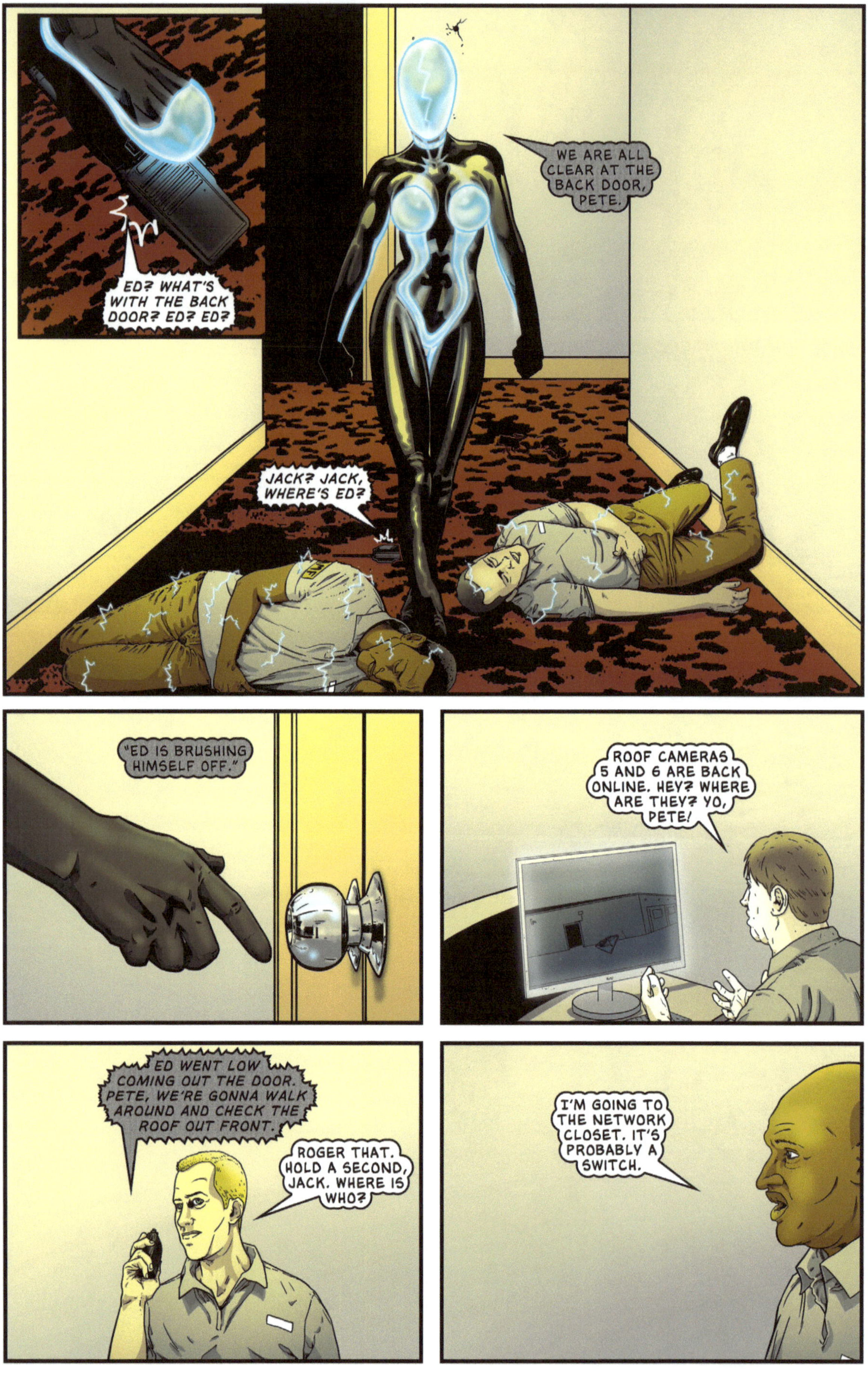

ED? WHAT'S WITH THE BACK DOOR? ED? ED?

WE ARE ALL CLEAR AT THE BACK DOOR, PETE.

JACK? JACK, WHERE'S ED?

"ED IS BRUSHING HIMSELF OFF."

ROOF CAMERAS 5 AND 6 ARE BACK ONLINE. HEY? WHERE ARE THEY? YO, PETE!

ED WENT LOW COMING OUT THE DOOR. PETE, WE'RE GONNA WALK AROUND AND CHECK THE ROOF OUT FRONT.

ROGER THAT. HOLD A SECOND, JACK. WHERE IS WHO?

I'M GOING TO THE NETWORK CLOSET. IT'S PROBABLY A SWITCH.

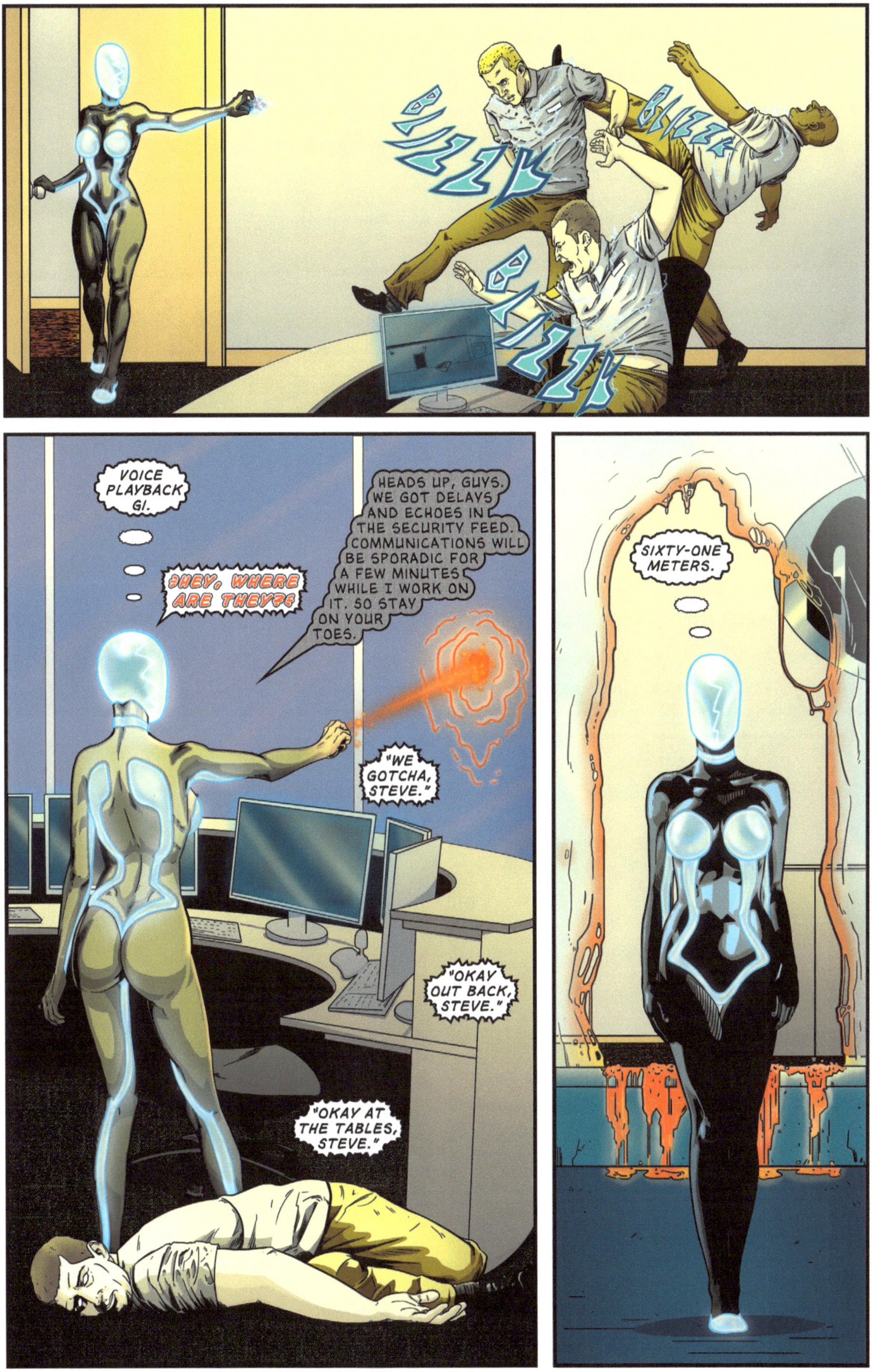

VOICE PLAYBACK GI.

"HEY, WHERE ARE THEY?"

HEADS UP, GUYS. WE GOT DELAYS AND ECHOES IN THE SECURITY FEED. COMMUNICATIONS WILL BE SPORADIC FOR A FEW MINUTES WHILE I WORK ON IT. SO STAY ON YOUR TOES.

"WE GOTCHA, STEVE."

"OKAY OUT BACK, STEVE."

"OKAY AT THE TABLES, STEVE."

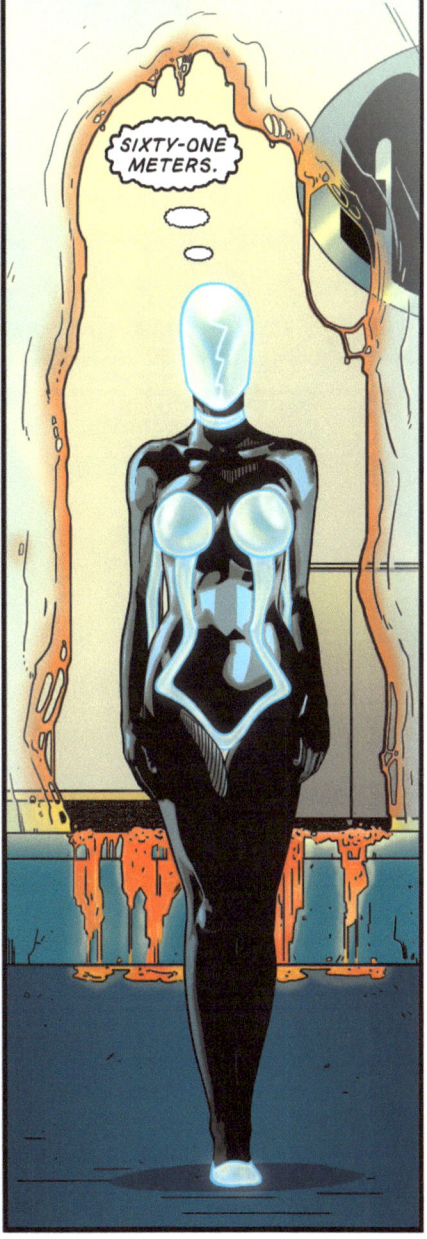

SIXTY-ONE METERS.

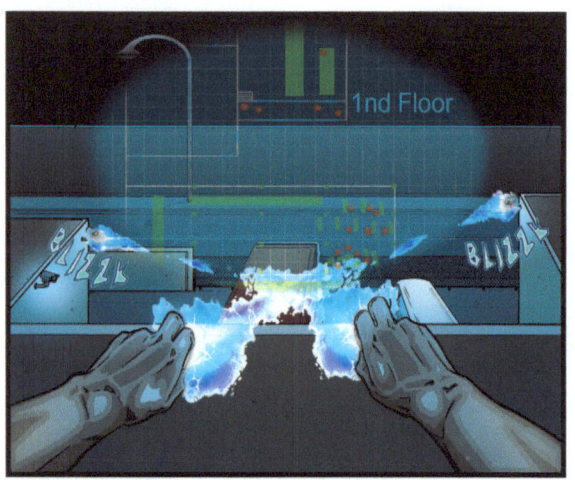

1nd Floor

IT'S AN ELECTRICAL SURGE.

BUT THE BUILDING IS GROUNDED.

STEVE, THE LOADING DOCK LIGHTS ARE BLOWING OUT. STEVE?

THAT BULB IS GOING TO POP.

VOICE PLAYBACK G4.

JACK, WHERE IS ED?

STEVE? STEVE?

STEVE SAID COMMUNICATIONS WOULD BE DOWN.

YEAH, HEY, THIS IS PETE. STEVE IS ON THE PHONE WITH THE ELECTRIC COMPANY. THERE IS A PROBLEM WITH OUR BUILDING'S POWER ON THEIR SIDE. STEVE SAYS LIGHTS WILL BE BACK ON IN A MINUTE.

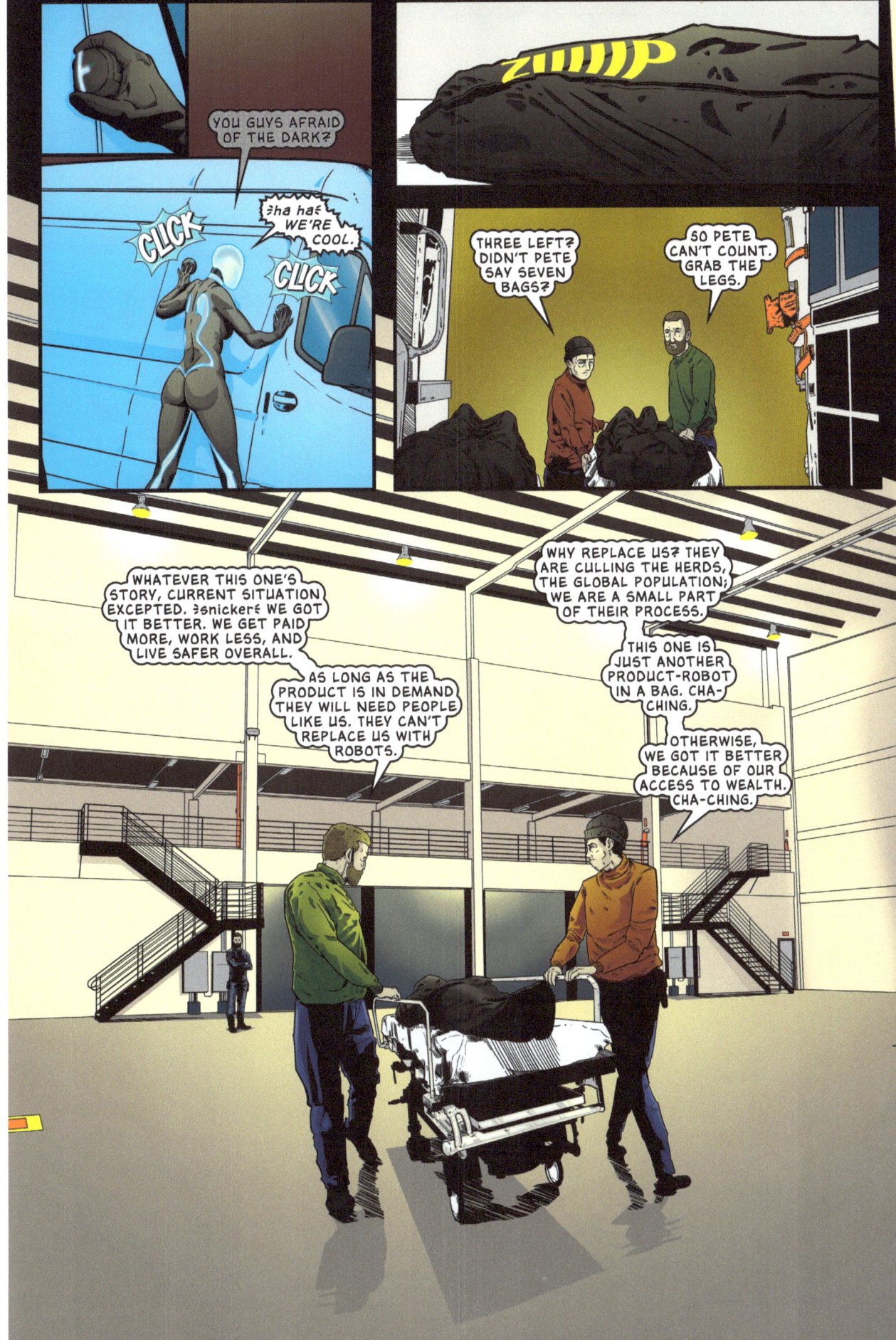

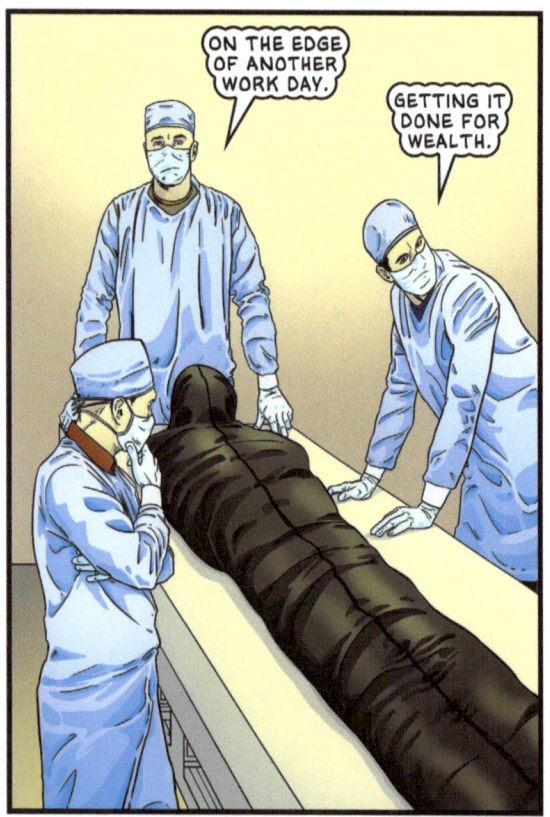

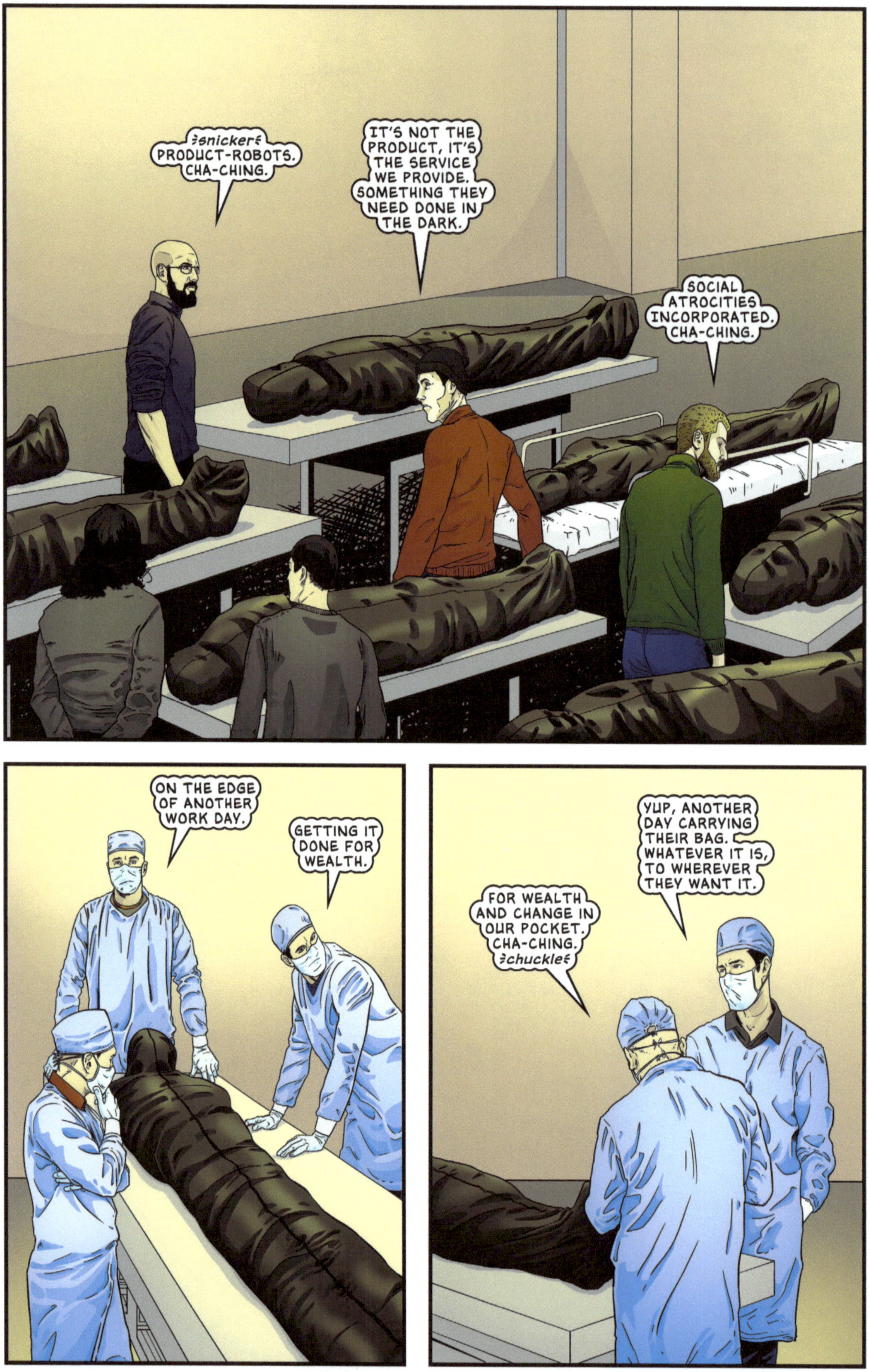

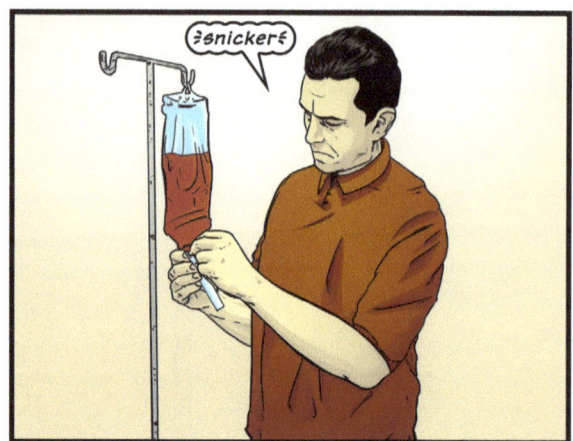

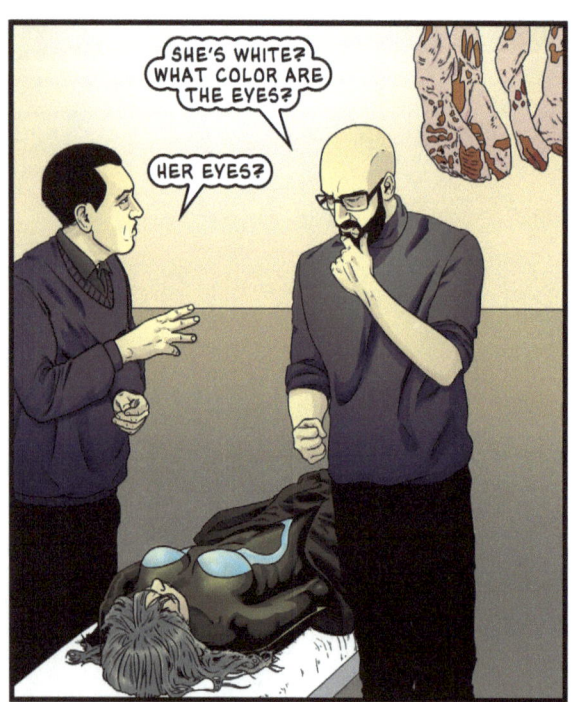

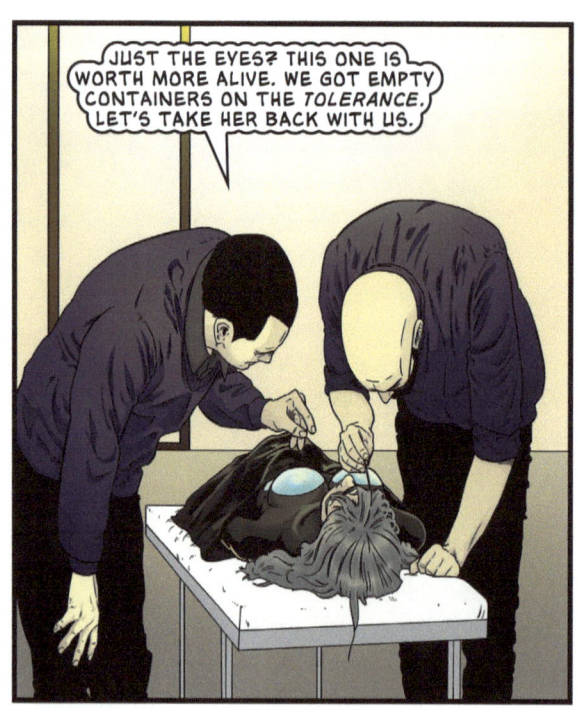

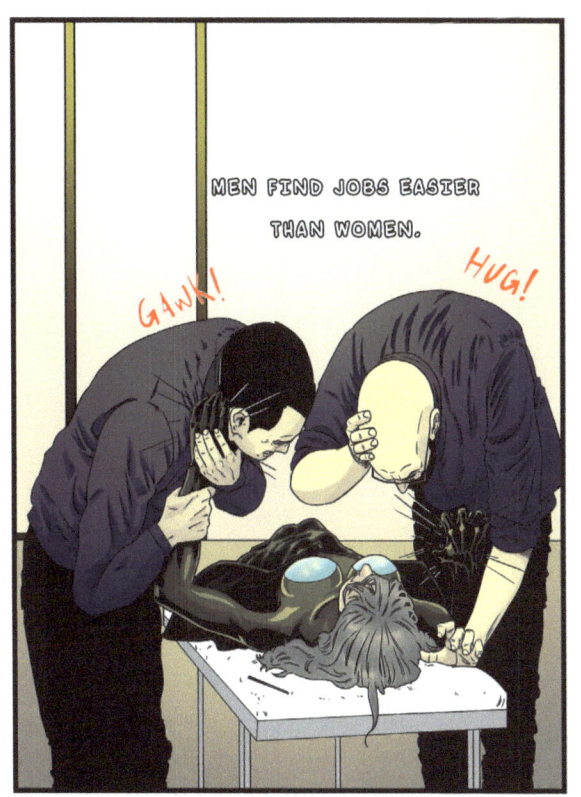

MEN FIND JOBS EASIER THAN WOMEN.

GAWK!

HUG!

UNLESS THE WOMAN IS SUITED FOR THE JOB.

HUG!

GAWK!

GIVEN THE SOCIETY, AS DETERMINED BY A MAN.

Arg!

ZAPP

THEY ARE CULLING THEIR HERDS, REDUCING THEIR POPULATIONS TO A MANAGEABLE SIZE...

CRACK!

TO PRESERVE AND HARVEST RESOURCES, AND ELIMINATE UNDESIRABLE TRAITS.

MALEFACTORS, IF ARRESTED, PENNED, MIGHT BE FREED OR ESCAPE,

POSSIBLY AID IN DISAPPEARING OTHERS.

THE OTHERS, THEM, JUST MORE OF THE MANY. THE MASSES, BORN INTO SITUATION, LIVING IN FEAR OF FRAILTY, FIXED IN BELIEF. LISTENING TO SELF-SATISFYING FALSEHOODS.

DIVORCED FROM THE INTIMACY OF TRUST.

CRACK!

EXPLOITING EACH OTHER'S NEEDS TO GAIN ADVANTAGE.

ZAP...

MORE SPACE. MORE TIME.

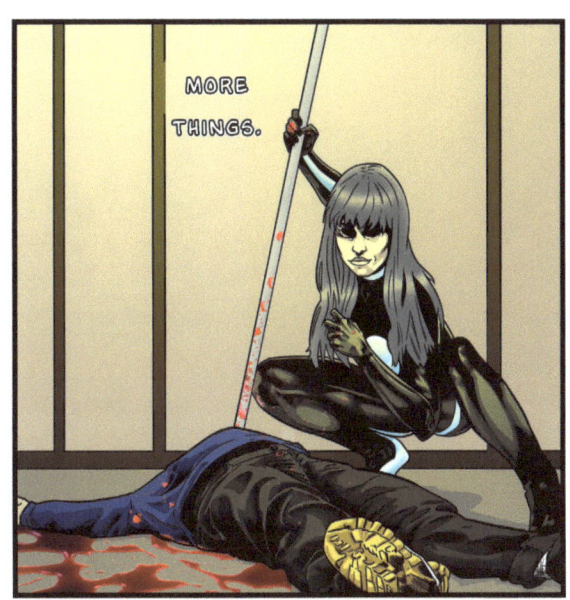

MORE THINGS.

JUST MORE OF THE MANY.

SOME MUST BE CHECKED.

KEPT IN THEIR PLACE.

TAUGHT TO SHOW RESPECT, TO KNOW THEIR PLACE.

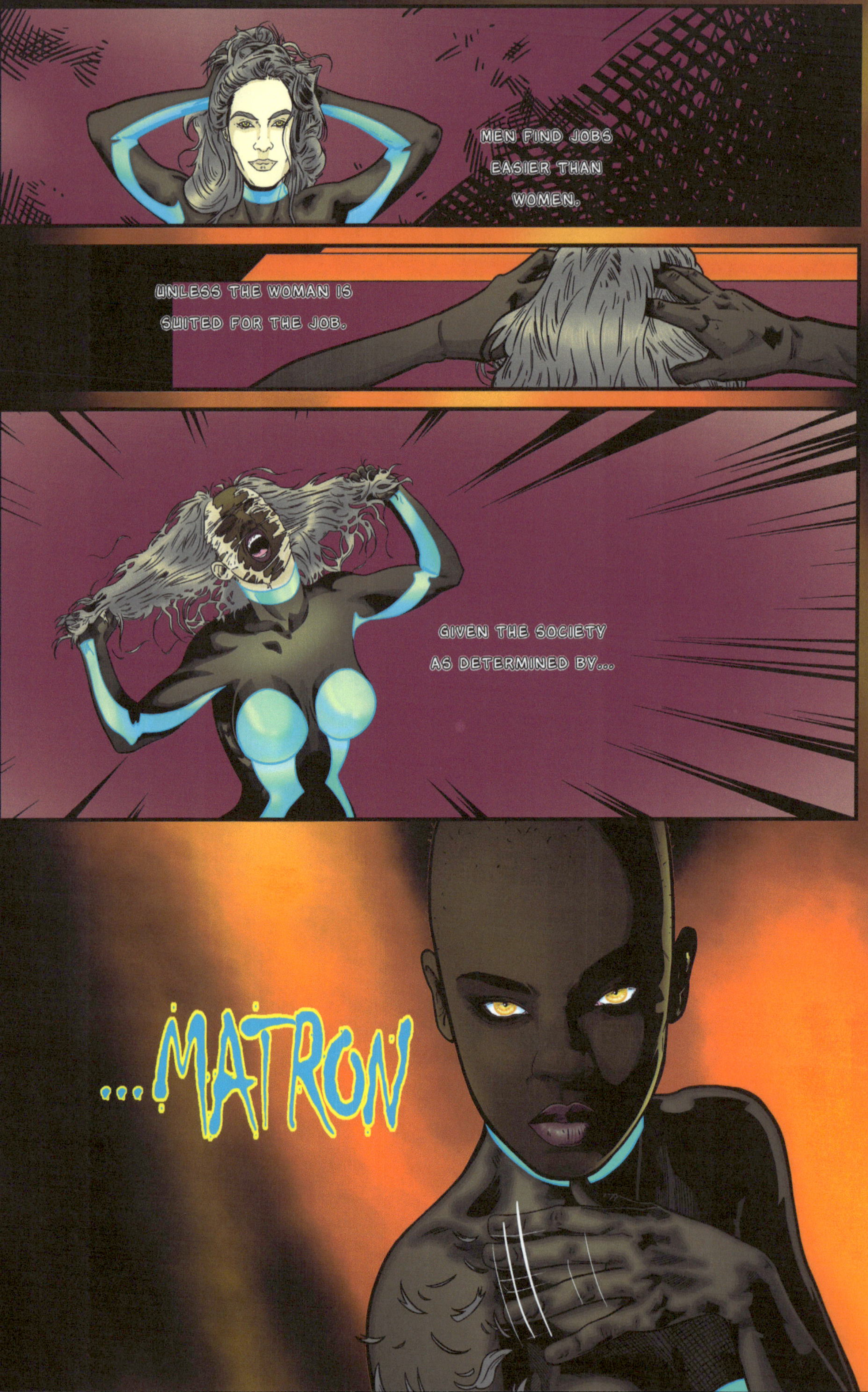

MEN FIND JOBS EASIER THAN WOMEN.

UNLESS THE WOMAN IS SUITED FOR THE JOB.

GIVEN THE SOCIETY AS DETERMINED BY...

...MATRON

HORSES, DOGS, WINE, BANANAS. BUILDING CORPORATIONS, INFLUENCING SOCIETIES. HOBBIES OF GENERATIONAL WEALTH.

USING LIFE FORMS AS MEDIUMS TO PASS TIME FOR ENTERTAINMENT AND PURPOSE.

CAPTAIN, WHEN MISS ORNEY ARRIVES BRING HER MOTORBIKE ONBOARD THEN GET UNDER WAY.

MATRON IS MOTORBIKING AROUND THE WORLD FOR FUN.

YES, IT IS NOT WORK.

MATTIE IS DOING WHAT SHE WANTS.

MATTIE DOES WHATEVER SHE WANTS.

AND ONLY WHAT SHE WANTS.

AND CAPTAIN, WE WILL BE DOCKING IN MIAMI.

AYE, AYE, SIR.

GENERATIONAL WEALTH,
JUST FAMILY GROUPS OF INDIVIDUALS
POSSESSING THE RESOURCES AND MEANS
TO PRODUCE THE BEST OF BREED
OR THE BEST VINTAGE.

PASSING ON THE
HOBBIES AND FREEDOM
TO DO WHAT THEY CHOOSE
FOR GENERATIONS.

...LEISURELY MATRON SAILS TO MIAMI, FLORIDA WITH ADEL FEISAL AND HIS WIVES. ALONG THE WAY MATRON GETS SCOLDED BY AN EX-LOVER ON THE MORALITY OF HER ACTIONS. ANXIOUS TO EXPERIENCE MIAMI MATRON RIDES OUT TO WHITE SHARKS RANCH TO MEET FORMER MIAMI WHITE SHARKS ALL-STAR QUARTERBACK, MIKE KERNS, OWNER OF AMF MEAT FRANCHISES AND *C.S. TOLERANCE.*

THERE IS A HOEDOWN IN THE BARN AT WHITE SHARKS RANCH CELEBRATING MIKE KERNS' INNOCENCE WHEN MIKE KERNS' SEXTING FRIEND LADY LIBERTY, A.K.A. EL, ARRIVES. FINALLY, THEY MEET IN THE FLESH FACE TO FACE...

NEXT EPISODE "STRAW TURKEY".

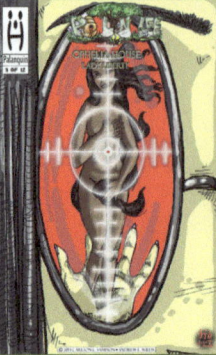

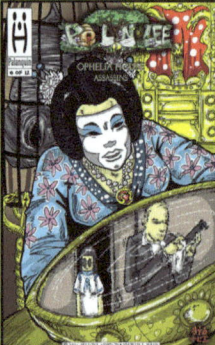

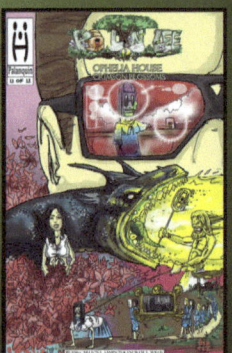

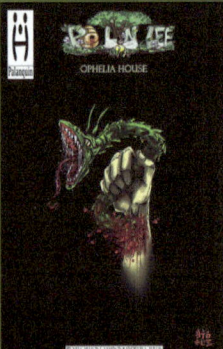

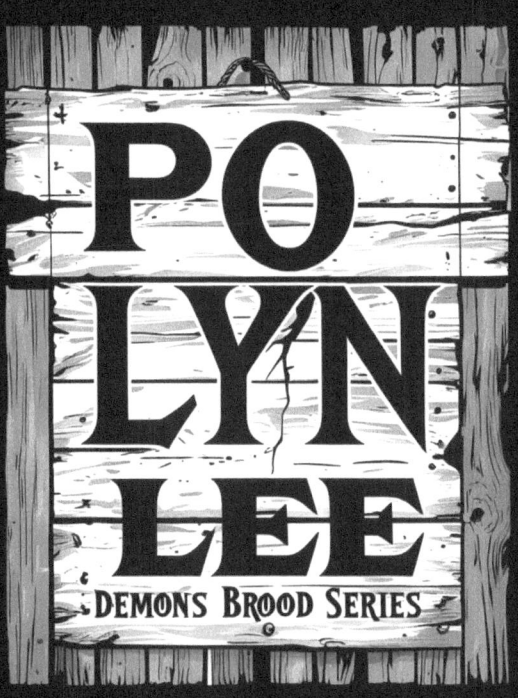

POLYN LEE

DEMONS BROOD SERIES

orneywines.com

thebookessence.com

thejerusalem14.com

polynlee.com

phascistclowns.com

oldmancupid.com

carltonlewissampson.com

ISBN 978-1-953132-04-8